BASEBALL
TURNAROUND

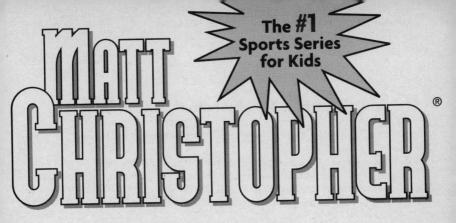

**The #1
Sports Series
for Kids**

Matt
CHRISTOPHER ®

BASEBALL
TURNAROUND

LITTLE, BROWN AND COMPANY

New York ❧ Boston

To Matthew F., who batted .300, at least

Little, Brown and Company

Hachette Book Group USA
237 Park Avenue , New York, NY 10017
Visit our Web site at www.lb-kids.com

www.mattchristopher.com

The characters and events portrayed in this book are fictitious. Any
similarity to real persons, living or dead, is coincidental and not
intended by the author.

Matt Christopher® is a registered trademark
of Matt Christopher Royalties, Inc.

Library of Congress Cataloging-in-Publication Data

Christopher, Matt
    Baseball turnaround / by Matt Christopher. — 1st ed.
        p.   cm.
    Summary: Sandy is drawn unknowingly into a shoplifting incident,
but when his community service involves his beloved baseball, he
meets people who help him finally put the past behind him.
    ISBN 978-0-316-14264-9
    [1. Baseball — Fiction.   2. Shoplifting — Fiction.]   1. Title
PZ7.C458Base   1997
[Fic] — dc21   96-53116

13 12 11 10 9

COM-MO

Printed in the United States of America

Prologue

The ball was coming straight toward him, right down the middle. It looked like it was doing ninety miles an hour. He had to go for it.

Sandy Comstock, center fielder for the Newtown Raptors, lifted his left foot, pulled his bat back, then swung at the round white missile.

Crack!

He felt the vibration of the bat as it hit the ball squarely and shot it into right field.

"Go, Sandy, go!"

"Dig it out! Dig! Dig!"

The cries from the bench and from the stands urged Sandy past first and on to second. He slid in a split second before the second baseman nabbed the throw-in.

"Safe!" the umpire called.

Sandy stood up and dusted off his pants, a wide grin on his face. Nothing felt better than playing good baseball on a sunny day. The past year had taught him that. It was something he hoped he'd never have to relearn, because it had been a painful lesson.

As he readied himself to react to the next play, he thought back to where he had been the year before. Back then, his jersey had read *Grantville Raiders*. Although it was only the next town over, Grantville seemed like a world away from Newtown.

There was no way to explain to anyone in Newtown what Grantville was like. Or what it had been like to grow up there. Newtown, with its neatly painted houses and freshly mowed lawns, sometimes seemed like another planet to him.

In Grantville, most of the houses were duplexes or triple-deckers split into apartments. Sandy's family had occupied a five-room apartment on the top floor of a three-story building that housed six other families. Besides the kitchen–dining room combo and living room, there were two bedrooms. One had been partitioned to make space for Sandy's twin sisters to sleep on one side. His bed was on the other.

With such cramped quarters, it was a relief to be outside. That's where Sandy and the other Grantville kids had spent most of their time. Only the worst weather kept them indoors. Instead they'd played on the streets and in the dusty backyards.

The only real patch of green worth playing on in Grantville was the ball field near the elementary school. Sandy had always loved the feel of the grass under his feet in early spring. He loved being out in the open space of the field with the warm sun blazing down on him. That was why he'd gone after an outfielder's slot on his first team.

It was hard to remember that he had come close to throwing all that away. But he had. And it would have been no one's fault but his own if he had lost it forever.

1

You're up first, right?" asked Skip Chessler, the Grantville Raiders' left fielder. He and Sandy were trotting toward the team dugout at the bottom of the final inning of their game with the Daytown Dazzlers. The Dazzlers had managed to hold on to a one-run lead as the game wound down to its conclusion.

"No, I'm on deck," said Sandy. "Billy leads off."

"That's a sure out," murmured Skip, taking his seat on the bench.

Sandy laughed harshly. "Yeah, but what can you do? He's our one southpaw pitcher. We gotta play him."

Billy Ligget had pitched a solid game, but his hitting wasn't as good. He made Sandy tense every time he came to the plate.

"Do your best, Billy," said Coach Samuels. "That's all I'm asking."

The rest of his team settled back to watch him fly, foul, or fan out in three pitches. Billy surprised everyone. He connected with the first pitch. The ball soared just over the head of the first baseman. It dropped in front of the right fielder, and Billy managed to trundle his way to first for a stand-up single.

The Raiders' fans went wild. Sandy Comstock, their leading hitter, was coming up next.

Sandy took a few swings with the two bats he'd been holding in the on-deck circle, then tossed one away. He strode to the plate, adjusted his batting helmet, and choked up on his bat. Then he narrowed his eyes and stared down the pitcher.

The Dazzler returned the stare, shook off two pitches, then reared back and released. It was a wild pitch coming straight at Sandy's head. Sandy jerked back. The catcher scrambled to retrieve the ball, then called time out.

"Tell your pitcher to watch it," Sandy muttered fiercely as the catcher started down toward the mound. He noted the catcher's look of surprise with satisfaction. *Bet he will tell him, too,* Sandy thought. *What a wimp.*

After time in, the next pitch started down the middle. But it curved midway and ended up well outside the strike zone.

"He's afraid of you!"

"Eye on the ball, Sandy!"

"You're ahead of him now!"

C'mon, give me something I can hit, Sandy thought, gritting his teeth. This time, the pitcher did. It was a little high and a little bit of a reach, but Sandy raised his bat and swung.

Crack!

Billy took off from first base as the ball soared into the air between center and left fields. It landed between the two outfielders, who both scrambled for it. Billy rounded second and made it safely to third moments before the ball thudded into the third baseman's mitt.

Sandy landed on second base with no trouble. He nodded over at Billy, who was giving him a thumbs-up sign. He didn't bother looking into the stands, though. He knew that no one from his family was there.

Skip, a solid hitter, was up next. Sandy took a few steps off the base, ready to sprint. *Hit it, Skip. Send me home so we can send these losers home.*

Four pitches came and went without a hit. Then, with a count of 2 and 2, Skip sent the next pitch out to the center field wall, just short of going over. He trotted down to first base as Billy, then Sandy, crossed home plate for the win.

The Raiders yelled and cheered.

"We showed them, didn't we? We sure showed them who was boss! They thought they could push us around, but we showed them," Sandy cried over and over. The ferocity in his voice drowned out all the others.

2

Sandy replayed each moment of the win on his way home. But once he walked up the steps to his family's apartment, he stopped thinking about it. It had been a long time since anyone here had asked him about baseball. He no longer tried to tell them about it.

He had barely set foot in the door when his mother shushed him.

"Shhhhh! Sandy, quiet!" she hissed, raising her finger to her lips. "The twins are asleep!"

She shut the door to the bedroom, then pulled him into the kitchen. Whispering, she explained.

"I don't think it's serious, but they both came home from school feeling sick to their stomachs," she said. "They looked flushed, too, so I took their temperatures. Margaret has a slight fever, but Mary's is normal. I put them to bed, and they just nodded off a few minutes ago."

"They don't sound so sick," said Sandy.

"No, and I'd like to keep it that way. So try not to make any noise," said Mrs. Comstock. "I have a million things to do before I get dinner going, so please don't bother me." She picked up the phone with one hand and shut the door to the small room she used as a study with the other.

Don't bother me. Try not to make any noise, Sandy mimicked to himself. *Whatever happened to "How was your day?"*

He dropped his school things next to the bedroom door. *So what am I supposed to do, anyhow? I can't move in this crummy apartment without bumping into something, and the walls are so thin I can practically hear the twins breathing.*

He stood for a moment, listening to his mother laughing on the phone. Then he left the apartment, resisting the temptation to slam the door after him.

The sun had dropped behind the treetops now. Although it was mid-spring, it was chilly outside.

9

Sandy tugged his Raiders baseball cap down lower over his ears. He decided to wait for his father to come home before going back inside.

There was only a fifty-fifty chance of that happening anytime soon. Mr. Comstock had been working extra hours for over a year now. Business at the trucking company that he managed was good, and, as he said, "You have to make it while you can." His overtime pay went into a special account — savings for a house someday, he told Sandy.

"Someday" seemed pretty far away.

Sandy slumped down on the steps in front of the apartment building. For a few minutes, he watched cars go by. But that was boring. He had to *do* something. He decided to take a walk to the convenience store and check out the magazines. He didn't have any money to buy anything, but using your eyes was free, wasn't it?

But when he got to the store, he had trouble getting near the magazines. A tough-looking group of kids was hanging out right in front of them. One of them, a muscular boy with red hair, seemed to be the leader. Sandy thought he looked a little familiar and wondered if he went to Grantville Middle School.

Sandy saw a magazine he wanted to look at, but the redhead was standing right in front of it. He tried to muscle his way to the sports rack, but the kid moved as if to block his path. Exasperated, Sandy finally just reached behind him. When he pulled the magazine free, his elbow brushed the kid in the head.

The redhead yelped and spun around, an angry look on his face. "Watch it!" he said dangerously.

"I barely touched you!" Sandy replied hotly.

The redhead narrowed his eyes. "Then I'll barely touch *you*," he said. With a lightning-quick move, he shoved Sandy backward. Hard.

Sandy careened into the rack. Magazines flew everywhere. The one in his hands tore in half as he tried in vain to keep from falling to the floor.

The store manager came running over. "Out! Out, all of you! I told you punks before to stay out of my store. I'm calling the cops if you don't leave." The boys made a few wisecracks, then split up and sauntered down the aisles. A few looked over their shoulders.

Sandy picked himself up, his baseball cap askew and the torn magazine still in his hands. "Give me that and get out," the store manager said angrily. "Go join your buddies and cause trouble elsewhere."

Sandy didn't bother telling the manager that the boys weren't his "buddies." He just hurried outside. He turned the corner toward home, then stopped short. There in his path stood the group of kids. The redhead stepped out in front of them.

Sandy tensed, his face forming a deep scowl. "What's the big idea?"

"Relax, baseball boy," the redhead said. "We just wanted to thank you."

"For what?"

The kid laughed harshly. "If you hadn't come along, we would have had to figure out a way to make off with all this stuff." After glancing around surreptitiously, each boy quickly showed Sandy items concealed in his jacket: a handful of magazines, a bag of candy, a bottle of soda. The redhead had a package of cigars. "Instead we had the perfect fall guy — you!"

Sandy blinked. "You stole that stuff?"

"We had to get supplies for our hangout. It's not

like our parents are going to give us money to pay for stuff like this, you know? That guy'll never miss it. And even if he does, we'll be long gone! But first —"

The redhead grabbed the magazines, leafed through them, then pulled one out. It was a copy of the same sports magazine Sandy had been reading. "Here, take it." He tossed it at Sandy.

Sandy looked at the magazine in his hands. Deep down, he knew what he should do — return the magazine and go home. But the store manager thought he was a "punk" and wouldn't believe him. And he wasn't about to let this gang see him making nice with someone who had insulted him.

"So what do you do with all this stuff?" he asked the redhead.

"We bring it back to our hangout and divvy it up. Why, you interested in seeing it firsthand?"

Sandy hesitated. Then he thought about what his mother had been like when he got home.

What the heck, he said to himself. *If I don't feel like sticking around, I'll just leave. At least I'll have something to do before dinner, whenever that's going to be.*

13

"Yeah, sure," he said. Then he stuffed the magazine in his back pocket and trailed behind the group.

The boys' hangout was nothing more than an abandoned storage shack behind one of the neighborhood apartment buildings. A rickety wooden table in the middle and a collection of old vegetable crates made up all the furniture. Piles of tattered magazines and newspapers were stacked in one corner. There were no windows or electricity, so one of the kids took some matches from his pocket and lit some candles.

The other boys joked about how they had fooled the store manager. Then they passed around the candy and opened the soda. The redhead lit one of the cigars and started puffing. Soon the others were doing the same. One offered Sandy a puff. When Sandy didn't take it, the redhead laughed his harsh laugh.

"Well, get *him*," he said to his buddies. "Thinks he's too good to give it a try. Is that it? Are you too good to give it a try, baseball boy?"

The taunts made Sandy angry. "I just remembered something I gotta do," he said, sidling around the table to the door. "See ya."

"What's the rush?" asked a tall boy with curly brown hair and a million freckles. He was one of the biggest of the kids. His body blocked the doorway.

"Gotta get home for dinner," said Sandy, suddenly uneasy.

"Oh, yeah? What's for dinner? Maybe we'll all come over and have some," said the redhead. The others all laughed at his suggestion.

"Yeah, right," said Sandy with a small laugh.

"Baseball boy's gotta keep his energy up so he can hit little white balls with sticks," said one of the other guys, giving Sandy a push as he passed by.

Automatically, Sandy pushed back at him. "Keep your hands off me," he warned.

"Aw, let him go," the redhead called over. "We already got what we needed out of him."

But the kid who had pushed him took another poke at Sandy's back. Sandy stumbled and collided with the table. The candles rocked dangerously.

Sandy's temper flared. He spun to face the boy who had pushed him. "I said, *Keep your hands off me.*" With one quick move, he pushed the big kid into the table and ran out the door. The boys followed him, shouting angry words and threats.

15

The noise brought people inside the apartments to their windows.

"That's it — I'm calling the cops!" one man yelled from his back stoop. He switched on an overhead light, reached into his doorway, and pulled out a phone.

Sandy rushed past him, giving the man a glance before disappearing into the shadows. Once there, he broke into a sprint. He didn't stop until he'd reached his own doorway. With shaking hands, he fumbled for the key.

That's when he heard the sirens and smelled the smoke.

3

Sandy, hat off at the dinner table," said Mrs. Comstock. "How many times do I have to tell you that?"

Sandy hung his Raiders cap from the back of his chair. He pushed his string beans around the crumbled remains of the slice of meat loaf on his plate. After the game, he had been so ravenous, he could have eaten a grizzly bear. Now he had no appetite.

Bzzing! Bzzinggg! The door buzzer sounded. Mrs. Comstock went to the speaker and pushed the button.

"Hello? . . . Yes. Yes, I'm his mother. . . . Yes. . . . Well, I suppose so. I mean, of course, please come up."

She turned to the table with a dark look on her

face. "Sandy, why would two police officers want to speak to you?"

Before he could answer, there was a knock on the door. A policeman in a blue uniform and one in ordinary clothes came into the living room. They introduced themselves as Officer Hughes and Lieutenant Nolan.

"I'll get right to the point," said Lieutenant Nolan. "Early this evening, there were two disturbances. The first was a robbery at the corner convenience store. The second was a fire. An old shack behind a building not too far from the store went up in flames. You were seen leaving both places."

Sandy stared at him, his heart in his mouth. "Me? What makes you think it was me?"

Lieutenant Nolan plucked the Raiders cap from the chair. "Not too many kids around with one of these. We got a roster of the team from the paper and a description of you from the witnesses. With the help of some team photos and newspaper clippings, we put two and two together."

His mother snapped, "Sandy, were you involved in this trouble?"

Sandy didn't look at her. "I guess I might have been."

"We have plenty of time," the policeman said. "Just tell us what happened."

Sandy knew he had to come clean. Starting with his meeting up with the kids at the convenience store, he gave them the bare facts. When he produced the magazine, he heard his mother take a sharp breath. Finally, he described the trip to the shack, making sure to mention that he had left as soon as he could.

"And there was a lot of noise afterward," he added. "But I don't know about any fire."

Then an image flashed through his mind: He was pushing the big kid into the table with the candles.

"I guess — maybe one of the candles could have been knocked over," he said lamely. "There was a lot of newspaper and stuff. Maybe it caught on fire."

"Candles and newspapers, huh?" Lieutenant Nolan wrote something in his notebook. "Can you tell us who the other boys were?"

Sandy hesitated. "No," he said. Lieutenant Nolan looked at him intently.

"You're sure about that? You don't sound too sure."

"Sandy," his mother warned, "if you know something else, tell the officers. Now."

Sandy sighed. "Well, one of the kids might go to Grantville Middle School. But I don't know his name."

"Uh-huh," said Officer Hughes. From a briefcase he was carrying, he pulled a book that Sandy recognized as the current edition of the Grantville yearbook. "Mind taking a look to see if you can identify this other boy?"

For the next ten minutes, Sandy sat with the volume in front of him, leafing through the pages. All at once he spotted the redhead. Even though the photo was black-and-white, he knew it was the same kid. *Perry Warden,* the caption read.

"That him?" Officer Hughes asked. Sandy nodded. "Fine. Well, we'll just ask you to write out a statement for now. If we need to get in touch again, we know where to find you."

A few minutes later, the policemen stood up to leave. Mrs. Comstock shot Sandy a look that spoke volumes.

The minute the door was closed, she picked up

his Raiders cap and faced him. "What's gotten into you? The way I see it, you've just made the last out of the game. Possession of stolen goods, strike one. Going off with strangers, strike two. Suspicion of arson, strike three. You're out!"

Sandy opened his mouth to explain but shut it again. *What's the use?* he thought. *She's going to believe what she wants to believe.* He picked up his book bag and stalked off to his room without a word.

Later that night, Sandy could hear his parents' whispers through his bedroom door. He couldn't make out what they were saying, but it didn't take much imagination to guess what it was about. Yet not in his wildest dreams had he expected to hear what he heard the next morning.

"Well, Sandy, we have some news for you. We had hoped to let you know this in a more upbeat way, but what you did has made us rethink that," his mother said. "So here it is: We're moving to a new house in Newtown at the end of next month. Because of what happened, we have decided that you should help us pack and mind the twins. So that means no more baseball. Talk to Coach Samuels today, tell him you have to quit the team, then come right home."

Sandy couldn't believe his ears. Moving? Quit the baseball team in mid-season "because of what happened"? As if what happened was all his fault! Without a word or a bite of breakfast, Sandy grabbed his book bag and rushed from the room. Frustration and anger clouded his eyesight. This time, he gave in to his temptation to slam the door.

4

School was a disaster that day. Everyone was buzzing about the fire — although as far as Sandy could tell, no one knew anything about his part in it. And he wanted to keep it that way.

So when he broke the news to Coach Samuels after school, he simply told him that his family was moving and that his parents needed his help with the preparations.

Coach Samuels sat back in his chair and sighed. "I can't say I'm happy to hear this news, Sandy," he said. "You're our number-one center fielder, and you're always a big help at the plate. But I can't argue with your parents' decision. So I'll shake your hand and wish you well."

And that was that. As the week progressed, talk of the trouble died down and Sandy was able to stick to his explanation that it was his parents' fault he was no longer on the Raiders. His teammates all expressed their anger and surprise, but none of them questioned his story.

Then, Thursday morning, a notice came to the Comstock household. It said that Sandy and his parents were to appear in Grantville Juvenile Court the following morning.

Sandy tucked his shirt into his trousers. His fingers stumbled as he buttoned the cuffs.

"Why's Sandy getting all dressed up?" asked Mary.

"He's going to jail," Margaret said, her mouth full of cereal.

"He is not!" said Mr. Comstock. "Sandy just has to go explain to the judge what happened. Then the judge will decide what to do."

"But I already told them everything I knew," Sandy protested.

"Officer Hughes told me that another boy is telling a different story."

Sandy was silent.

"Do you have to stand up in court and swear to tell the truth?" asked Mary.

Mrs. Comstock said, "Will you girls please hurry up so we can drive you to school!"

The two seven-year-olds pestered Sandy all the way to their school. When they finally arrived at the school yard, Mary asked one last question: "Who is the other boy who says you're not telling the truth?" Sandy had no answer for that. But he had a good idea he knew who it was: Perry Warden.

The rest of the ride to the juvenile court was quiet. Sandy kept going over what happened in his mind. Could he have knocked over the candles? Would he be considered a shoplifter for not returning the magazine even though he hadn't taken it?

What would the judge think? Would his friends at school find out?

As they walked up the steps to the courthouse, Sandy steeled himself. With a deep breath, he pushed the doors open and walked into the courtroom.

His courage faltered when he saw who was inside the hearing room. It was the redhead, Perry Warden. He glared at Sandy, then turned away.

The judge came in and sat down, then took up a stack of papers from his desk. "I've read all the statements, the police and the eyewitness reports, and someone is definitely not telling the truth. So, I'll give you both one last chance to do the right thing. First, the store manager's allegation of theft. Anyone willing to own up to that?"

There was a long pause. All Sandy could hear was the whir of the ceiling fan going round and round. Out of the corner of his eye, Sandy saw Perry Warden glance over at him. Sandy refused to look at him. Instead, at a prodding from his father, he stood up and repeated to the judge all that he had told the police officers. He could feel the redhead's eyes burning a hole in his back when he sat back down.

"Well, Mr. Comstock, you are in luck," the judge said. "The store manager is willing to drop the charges if he receives proper payment for the items taken by the end of the day. Although the manager identified Mr. Warden here by his red hair, you were the only one found in actual possession of the stolen goods. So the burden of payment is on you. I trust that won't be a problem? Good." He consulted his papers again.

"All right," said the judge with a sigh. "What about

this fire? Says probable cause was candles and news-papers. Mr. Comstock? Mr. Warden?"

This time, Sandy stayed seated. He still didn't know if he had caused the fire. And he wasn't about to take the blame for something that couldn't be proven.

"I see," said the judge. "Well, then, I'll have to rule on the evidence I do have. Fortunately, the owner of the abandoned shack has asked for no restitution since the building destroyed was of no real value."

Sandy wanted to shout for joy until the judge continued. "But the community was endangered by reckless behavior. Mr. Comstock, you were posi-tively identified as being near the fire and you yourself have admitted that you were there. Mr. Warden, your red hair gave you away again; you, too, were identified. Since your two stories don't match up and no new evidence is likely to come to light, I'm holding you both responsible. You're on probation for the next six weeks. During that time, you will be required to perform twenty hours of community service and you will report regularly to your probation officer. When you have fulfilled these requirements to the satisfaction of the court, this incident will be expunged from the record. Is that clear?"

There was a murmur of assent throughout the courtroom.

"All right, then, you are free to go."

There was a shuffle as everyone stood up to leave. As Sandy passed Perry Warden, he heard the other boy hiss, "Snitch. I'll get you for this."

Sandy scowled but didn't say a word. All he wanted to do was leave the courtroom.

Mr. and Mrs. Comstock registered Sandy for his first appointment with his probation officer, then walked with him out to the car. But his father didn't start the engine right away.

"All things considered, that wasn't too bad," said Mr. Comstock. "I mean, let's face it — you were somewhere you shouldn't have been."

"Twenty hours of community service seems like a bargain price to pay to have your record cleared," added Mrs. Comstock.

Sandy just looked out the window.

Mrs. Comstock sighed. "Look at it this way, Sandy.

We'll be in Newtown in a few more weeks. No one there knows anything about this. We can all just put it behind us. Until then, you're going to have to deal with whatever backlash comes your way."

As they drove into the Grantville Middle School parking lot, Sandy couldn't help wonder what form that "backlash" might take. He didn't have to wait long to find out.

5

Sandy arrived at school in time for lunch. As usual, he sat with some of the guys from the team. As he took his chair, some of them looked at him a little funny.

"What?" he asked. "Can't a guy be late one day?"

Timmy Phelps, the Raiders' catcher, swallowed his hunk of chicken salad sandwich and blurted out, "So what happened, you know, this morning? Did you get in big trouble in juvenile court 'cause of the shed fire? Did you really steal that stuff?"

"Yeah, we just heard that a perpetrator wearing a Raiders cap was arrested for the shack fire. Was it you? Is that why you quit the team?" said Skip. The other boys gave Sandy sidelong looks.

Sandy turned red. "Who'd you hear that from?"

"Some kid with red hair told another kid who told Timmy."

"And Timmy just couldn't wait to tell you guys, I bet," Sandy retorted, his temper rising. "I would have thought you guys would believe me over some rumor! Do I look like a criminal to you? No. So why don't you all just leave me alone?"

He grabbed up the rest of his lunch and moved to another table across the room. *They've already decided that I'm a juvenile delinquent! Well, who cares what they think. And what's with that Perry Warden, spreading rumors about me?*

No one came near him. They just finished eating lunch and left the table as quickly as possible.

On his way out, Timmy said to Sandy, "Sorry if I said anything that made you mad."

"Yeah, well, I'll get over it. Don't forget — I'm moving out of this stupid town at the end of the school year. Then maybe I'll find some real friends."

Timmy didn't say a word. He hurried away to join the other boys. Sandy watched as he tugged on Skip's arm and muttered something in his ear.

Sandy fumed about the cafeteria incident for the

rest of the school day. When he was at his locker after the last bell, he overheard a group of girls making plans to attend the Raiders baseball game. He slammed his locker shut and stormed down the hall to get away from them.

"Whoa, what's eating him?" he heard one girl say.

"Didn't you hear?" another said. "He got kicked off the team because he's an arsonist and a shoplifter!"

Sandy had never been so happy to be in the apartment as he was that night. He helped his parents pack up books, paintings, toys, and other items they weren't going to need until they got to their new house.

When he climbed into bed, he said a silent prayer of thanks that the next day was Saturday so he didn't have to go to school. Then he remembered that he was meeting with his probation officer first thing in the morning.

Saturday was warm and sunny, without a cloud in the sky. Normally on a day like this, Sandy would be out playing ball with the rest of the guys. But all that was different now.

It took Sandy and his mom less than twenty minutes by car to get to the big brick building where he had his appointment. But it was another ten minutes before he was asked to go inside for his first meeting with Stan Richards, the probation officer.

He slumped in a chair across from the officer's desk, eyes down on his toes. He looked up only after Mr. Richards cleared his throat.

"So, looks like you got mixed up in a bit of trouble. Have you looked into your community service yet?"

"No," Sandy told him. "And I don't know if I should even look for something around here." He explained that his family was moving.

"Moving, eh? How do you feel about that?" Mr. Richards asked.

"How do I feel?" he replied. "I feel fine about it. It's getting me out of this lousy town, anyway." He couldn't stop the bitterness from entering in his voice.

Mr. Richards cocked an eyebrow. "Things been a little rough lately?"

Sandy shifted in his chair. "Yeah, you could say that — if you call being wrongly accused of arson and theft, finding out your so-called friends are rats, and being forced to quit the baseball team all in one week 'rough,'" he said sourly.

"Baseball, huh? I'm a fan of baseball myself," Mr. Richards replied mildly. "Maybe we can find you some community service that has to do with baseball."

Sandy looked at the probation officer for the first time. "What would I have to do?" he asked.

Mr. Richards kept talking as if Sandy hadn't spoken. "I have to warn you, though, if I hook you up with the job I'm thinking of, you're going to have to lose the bad attitude I'm hearing from you. You've got a lot of resentment churning around inside you because of what's happened. Maybe it goes back before then, even. Whatever the case, this job isn't the place for a guy with a chip on his shoulder."

Sandy was silent.

"Tell you what," Mr. Richards continued. "We'll give you a trial run. Meet me tomorrow at Begley Field. You'll try the job for an hour, then we'll decide if it will work. That hour will count toward the twenty you owe us. Oh, and bring your glove. Okay?"

Sandy nodded.

"By the way, Sandy, what did you tell your coach about quitting the baseball team?"

"He thinks it's because we're moving. The kids at school think that, too." *Or they used to before Perry Warden interfered,* he added silently.

Mr. Richards tapped his pencil on his desk. "You know, sooner or later, stories about the incidents are going to surface. You might be better off being up front with people right from the start."

Sandy shook his head. "The way I see it, I'm out of this town. Then anyone can say anything he wants to about me. It won't matter."

Mr. Richards didn't say anything to that. The meeting ended a few minutes later. Sandy went outside to the waiting car.

"How did it go?" his mother asked.

"Okay," said Sandy. "I think I have a job."

6

The next day, Sandy arrived at Begley Field at the appointed time. The field was located on the town line between Newtown and Grantville and was a short bike ride from his house. Two minutes later, Mr. Richards drove up. Someone was in the car with him.

"Sandy, I'd like you to meet my brother, Lou," Mr. Richards said. "I told him about you, and he thinks he might be able to use you."

"You see, I need a little help coaching baseball," Mr. Lou Richards added.

Sandy's eyebrows shot up. "Coaching? Coaching who?"

"I coach a team for the Police Athletic League. Most of the players haven't had much experience with baseball, but they're trying to get better. I need volunteers to help them work on the rules, on their batting, and things like that. Think you could do that?"

"I don't know if I could, but I guess I could try," said Sandy.

"All right then, let's see what you can do." Coach Richards opened the trunk of the car and pulled out a bat, ball, and two gloves. He also had three baseball caps with the name *Dolphins* printed on them. He gave one to Sandy.

"Head out into the field and see what you can do with these hits," he instructed. "You, too, Stan. No slackers on a day like today."

Obediently, Mr. Richards and Sandy jogged onto the field. Coach Richards started hitting high fly balls. Sandy was a little rusty at first, but soon he was back in the groove and having a good time.

"Next drill!" called Coach Richards. "Three-way catch. Heads up, Sandy!" A fireball blazed toward Sandy. But he caught it with ease and rifled it to Mr. Richards in a flash. The ball went round and round among them, then zigzagged at random. Sandy had to work hard to keep up. And to his surprise, he found that he was beginning to enjoy himself.

"Last but not least, let's see your hitting power. Stan, you play the field. Sandy, I'm going to pitch you some. Try hitting them all over. My brother needs some exercise."

For the first time in days, Sandy cracked a smile. Twenty minutes later, Mr. Richards trotted in from the field. "Enough, already. If I have to sprint the width of the field one more time, I'm going to expire."

"Well, Sandy," said Coach Richards, chuckling, "that's all the proof I need. You can play the game, and I'm willing to take a chance that you can coach it, too. If you want to give me some time, I'd like to have you help out."

"Only twenty hours, though, right?" Sandy asked.

Mr. Richards checked his watch. "Nineteen, actually."

Sandy nodded. "Okay, you got a deal."

"All right, then, the team meets right here," said Coach Richards. "Every Tuesday and Thursday from two-thirty to four. You can use your school pass on the bus to get there and back. That's true from both Grantville and Newtown, by the way. Oh, and if your parents want to know anything about this, ask them to give me a call. Here's the number."

Sandy took the piece of paper Coach Richards handed to him and shoved it in his pocket.

"I'll give it to them, but I doubt they'll be calling you. They don't really care about baseball," said Sandy.

The brothers exchanged a look. Coach Richards shrugged. "I see. Well, maybe they'll change their minds. See you on Tuesday."

They waved to him and walked off.

Sandy looked after them for a long time. Then he unlocked his bike and headed home.

On Tuesday, Sandy brought his glove and his new Dolphins hat with him to school, along with a change of clothes. When the final bell rang, he ran quickly to the gym locker room and switched into his sweats. He wanted to be out before the baseball team came in. But he didn't make it. Timmy Phelps came in just as he was leaving.

"Dolphins?" said Timmy, pointing to Sandy's hat. "Who are they?"

"Just some team I'm coaching," Sandy replied. "And I'm late, so look out." He pushed by Timmy, who called out, "How come you have time to coach but not to play for the Raiders? I bet that's not even what you're really doing!"

Sandy just kept on walking. *Who needs you!* he fumed. *I can't wait to get out of this town.*

Timmy's comment rattled in his head the whole bus ride to Begley Field. By the time he got there, he was ready to slug more than one baseball out into deep center field.

Then he remembered what Mr. Richards had said: He wouldn't be right for this job if he let his temper get in the way. And when he caught sight of the members of the Dolphins team, he thought he understood why.

Seated in a semicircle around Coach Richards was a ragtag group of kids, none of whom looked older than ten. In the parking lot behind them was a minivan with the lettering *Grantville Homeless Shelter* on the side.

Coach Richards waved Sandy over. When the kids turned their faces up to him, his anger started to fade. They all looked so eager to learn.

"How many of you have played the game?" Coach Richards asked the kids.

A few hands were raised in the air.

"A real game on an actual field with uniforms and protective helmets?"

There were no hands raised now.

"I thought so," said Mr. Richards. "Well, this is Sandy. He's played a lot of baseball, and he's here to help us out. So half of you grab a glove and stay with him. He's going to talk with you about the game. The other half, I'm going to take over there" — he pointed to the batting cage — "and we're going to see how well you can hit a ball. After a while Sandy and I will swap groups."

And so it began. After a few hesitant starts, Sandy found himself talking easily to his group about the rules of the game. Most of them wanted to do nothing but hit the ball. Then Sandy explained how satisfying it could be to make a play, tag someone out, or make a tough catch. After that, they peppered him with questions.

When their interest waned, he told them about some of his games with the Raiders.

"So why aren't you playing now?" asked a little girl nicknamed Newt. "Why are you here with us?"

41

"That's none of your business!" snapped Sandy. The girl recoiled, tugged her hat low over her eyes, and held her glove up to her face.

Sandy wished he could pull the words back into his mouth. "Newt, listen, I didn't mean anything by that. Come on, put your glove down. How do you expect to catch any fly balls holding it like that?"

The girl slowly lowered her glove and peeked out from under her hat. Sandy gave her a half smile that turned into a full grin when she smiled back.

Gotta watch that, Comstock, he reprimanded himself. *Coach Richards might decide you're too hot-headed for the job, and then where will you be? It may not be the Raiders, but at least you're on the ball field instead of back in the apartment with boxes, tape, and twins!*

Still, by the end of the hour-and-a-half session, he was ready to head home. Coaching was harder work and the kids more demanding than he had thought they'd be. The team wasn't much good, either. Yet to his surprise, he was looking forward to the next practice.

He came back that Thursday afternoon and the following Tuesday and Thursday as well. On Wednesdays, he met with Mr. Richards to give him an update and record his hours. Mr. Richards listened with such interest that Sandy found himself talking about much more than just the coaching job. The attitude of the kids at school, wanting to keep what had happened a secret, and problems with his parents all came up.

Mr. Richards told him again and again, "You just have to deal with the situations as best you can — head on, honestly, and directly is always better than avoiding them, I think."

Sandy half-wished that he could follow that advice. But his former teammates were barely talking to him anymore. His parents were so wrapped up in final preparations for the move that he couldn't get a word in edgewise. And as for being honest about what had happened, forget that!

His only bright spot during the last week of school was that he hadn't run into Perry Warden in the school halls. When Sandy closed his locker for the last time, he breathed a sigh of relief.

Good-bye, Grantville. Hello, Newtown! he thought. *Where no one knows who I am or what I did. Or ever will.*

7

The next day, Saturday, the Dolphins had their first scheduled game. Sandy tugged on his team T-shirt and put on his cap. He was ready.

"Sorry we can't come see your team in action, Sandy," Mrs. Comstock said. "But the movers will be here any minute. We'll pick you up afterward, though. I'd hate for you to get lost trying to find the house."

The Comstock household had been in total chaos for two weeks. Everything that could be packed or dismantled was stacked in one corner of the apartment. The whole family had been sleeping on mattresses on the floor, pulling clothes out of suitcases, and eating with plastic utensils and paper plates. Now at last they were moving to their new home.

Sandy had noticed that the closer to moving day

they got, the cheerier his mother and father were. They were still too busy to talk about anything but packing and moving, but their good moods were infectious. Sandy had started playing with the twins, hiding in the big cardboard boxes, then jumping out and scaring them until they dissolved into giggles.

Sandy and the twins had first seen the house in Newtown a week and a half earlier. It was two stories, had a big backyard, a garage, and a huge basement. Sandy had his own room upstairs, the twins were across the hall in a room together, and in between was the bathroom. Mr. and Mrs. Comstock's room was downstairs, with their own bathroom. There was a separate kitchen, living room, dining room, and even a small TV room. To Sandy, it looked like a palace after the cramped apartment.

Now Sandy pulled his bike up from the basement storage room. "Okay, Mom, I'll look for you after the game," he called up to the apartment. "And sorry I can't help with the moving."

Mrs. Comstock wrestled a box down the stairs. "Oh, I'm sure you're *really* sorry," she said, puffing and putting the box down with a groan. "But don't you worry, there will be plenty of *unpacking* waiting for you at the other end!" She ruffled Sandy's hair, something she hadn't done for a long time. It made Sandy realize again just how happy she was they were moving.

The Dolphins were already on the field warming up when he pedaled up. "Hi, Coach!" squeaked Newt, the Dolphins' first baseman. "I'm so nervous I feel like I have to pee all the time!"

Sandy laughed. Over the last two weeks, he'd grown a soft spot in his heart for the small girl. "Listen, Newt," he replied, "you don't have anything to be nervous about. You just go out there and play a good game. That's all anyone can do, right?"

"Right!"

Still, he had to admit that he was feeling a little nervous himself. After all, no matter how talented the players were, a ball team was only as good as the coaching it received. Even though he was only here because he had to be, he'd hate to feel he'd let the little players down.

The opposing team, the Leopards, arrived ten minutes later. They were sponsored by the library and had use of the library's minivan. The kids tumbled out, yelling encouragement to one another.

Their head coach hopped out of the driver's seat. Then an older boy emerged from the passenger's side.

Sandy's stomach flip-flopped when he recognized the boy. Even though he couldn't see his hair, it was a face he wouldn't soon forget. Perry Warden!

Perry spotted him a second later. Sandy saw him scowl, then heard him yell to one of his players to come get the equipment bag. The player jumped as if he'd been stuck by a pin and hurried to help.

The two head coaches met to shake hands and greet the umpires. Coach Richards came back to the Dolphins dugout grinning.

"I think we're in for a good match today, Sandy!" he said. "It should prove to be interesting."

Sandy wondered if the coach knew who the Leopards' assistant coach was. If he did, he didn't let on. So even though he felt like a long-tailed cat in a room full of rocking chairs, Sandy returned the coach's smile and gave him a thumbs-up sign. There was no way he was going to show him the tension he felt at the sight of Perry Warden.

The Dolphins were up first.

"Come on, Manning! Let's go, Willoughby!" Sandy

called from his coaching spot next to third base. As each batter stepped up to the plate, Sandy cheered him or her on. And whether the kids hit the ball or not, he had nothing but praise for them when they got on base or headed back to the dugout.

"Nice going, Styles!" or "You'll get 'em next time, Wallace!" he cried.

Giving such positive encouragement was new to Sandy. At the beginning of the season, he had criticized a few of the kids and chewed out one boy for missing an easy catch. It was how he used to talk when he played for the Raiders.

But somehow, he never felt quite right saying the same kinds of things here. Then one scrimmage, he had listened closely to Coach Richards. The coach found something good to say to everyone. The next practice, Sandy followed his lead. To his surprise, the kids played better than they had when he'd yelled at them.

Apparently, that wasn't something the Leopards' assistant coach had picked up on. Every word out of his mouth was a slam. And he didn't limit his comments to his own team; more often than not, he ridiculed the Dolphins.

"C'mon, you Leopards, tear these slimy fish apart! They're nothing!"

And after a Dolphin outfielder had dropped a ball: "Hey, Dolphins, didn't your coaches teach you how to retrieve the ball? Try doing it with your snouts next time!"

Sandy ignored him as best he could. But one comment above all the others stuck in his craw. A Leopard runner had missed tagging second base on his way to third. Both Sandy and the second baseman had spotted it. Sandy called a time out and brought it to the attention of the umpire. The second baseman pointed out the shoe mark three inches away from the base.

"I'm sorry," the ump said to the Leopards' head coach. "It's just too obvious to let go by."

On the sidelines, Perry Warden looked disgusted, then yelled, "Shake it off, Leopards! These guys snitch all the time! They can't let anything go by without whining about it!"

Sandy knew the comment was directed at him. He turned beet red as his temper flared up.

That kid is asking for it, he thought fiercely. Then he glanced over at Coach Richards. The coach was frowning slightly, but he only clapped his hands and shouted, "Good eye out there, good eye. Let's keep it going, Dolphins!"

Sandy swallowed his anger as best he could and turned his attention back to the game.

At the end of the sixth inning, the score was tied. The two coaches announced that normally they would go into extra innings. But since this was their first game of the season and it was getting dark, they were going to call it a tie and let it go at that.

It was with great relief that Sandy watched Perry Warden climb into the minivan and ride away.

Coach Richards came over to him as they got ready to leave.

"So, how did it feel to coach your first game?" he asked.

"It's great," Sandy admitted.

"Yeah, I love watching the kids' enthusiasm for the game grow. I've always felt that was more important than winning or losing — although some coaches seem more intent on pushing their kids to win at any cost." He gave Sandy a sidelong glance. "I'm glad to see you're not one of those kind."

Sandy returned his look.

"I guess coaching has given me a different angle on the game," he said thoughtfully "Someday I'd really like to go into it."

"Someday, huh? Let me guess, you'd rather be playing, right?" asked the coach.

Sandy nodded.

"Thought you'd say that. In fact, I've been wondering if you'd seen the notice in the newspaper about the Newtown summer league that's starting up next week."

Sandy hadn't.

"It could be a good way for you to meet a bunch of kids in Newtown," the coach continued. "The teams are sponsored by local companies. They hold regular practices and games." He told him the date and time for sign-ups.

"Oh, and Sandy, one more thing. I know that you're only coaching with me to fulfill your community service. For what it's worth, I'd like you to keep on after your twenty hours are up. The kids like you, and it's only until the end of June, anyway. What's three more weeks?"

Sandy didn't hesitate. "It's a deal," he said.

Coach Richards broke into a big smile. "Hoped you'd say that" was his only reply.

While Sandy helped pick up after the game, he thought about what the coach had said about the summer league. It would be a good way to meet some guys, he supposed. And the idea of being on a brand-new team where no one knew anything about him was definitely appealing.

When his mother picked him up, he told her about the league. "I think I'd like to join it, if it's okay with you and Dad."

His mother glanced at him and smiled. "Sandy," she said, "I'm glad to hear that you want to look into this. It seems strange to not have you playing like you used to."

Sandy looked at her with surprise.

"I know, I know," she said in answer to his unasked question. "Your father and I kind of lost touch with your baseball last year. But we want to make up for it if we can. This will be a good way for us to start."

Sandy felt a warm rush of happiness flood through him. That feeling stayed with him as the car turned into the driveway of the Comstocks' new house. He was about to get out of the car when his mother took hold of his hand.

"Welcome home, son," she said softly.

Sandy nodded thoughtfully. "Thanks, Mom," he said. "I think it's going to be really great living here. Really great."

8

The next Wednesday, Sandy was leaving Mr. Richards's office after his regular appointment. He was in a good mood; he was just about halfway through his community service requirement. Mr. Richards had praised him for his decision to continue on with the Dolphins, too.

But the minute Sandy walked out the door, his mood changed drastically. Seated in a chair outside another probation officer's door was Perry Warden.

The redhead narrowed his eyes, then glanced down the hall, stood up, and sauntered over to Sandy.

"Well, if it isn't the snitch. I've been wondering where you've been hiding. Under some rock, I'll bet, or in some slimy dark corner with the other rats."

Sandy tried to push past the boy, but Perry shifted so he was again in front of him. "What's the matter? Aren't you glad to see me?"

"Listen, just leave me alone, okay? I'm not looking for any trouble," Sandy muttered.

"Yeah, well, maybe trouble will find you anyway. I'm keeping my eye on you, Comstock."

The probation officer's door opened just then. "You'll have to excuse me for now," Perry said. "Thanks to you, I have an appointment that can't be missed."

Perry gave Sandy one last glance. Then he strode into the office.

Sandy tried to put the incident out of his mind by focusing on the upcoming sign-ups for the summer league. When the time came, he was among the first in line.

He gave the man at the desk his name, told him he was fourteen years old, and that he had played baseball since he was eight. The man handed him a cap and a T-shirt with the name *Raptors* emblazoned on it.

"That'll be your team. Be sure to pick up the

practice and game schedule in the envelope at the end of the desk."

Sandy did as he was told. He glanced at the schedule and saw that the first practice was in two days' time. The team practiced in the early evening, from four-thirty until six-thirty, so he wouldn't have to miss any Dolphins practices. Shoving the paper into his back pocket, he headed for the door.

On his way out, he bumped into a burly boy with a crew cut. He apologized and was about to move away, when the boy caught his arm.

"Raptors, huh?" the boy said, looking at the shirt in Sandy's hand. "I was the Raptors' catcher last year and should be again this year. Guess that'll make us teammates."

The boy introduced himself as Ben Eaton. They shook hands, and Sandy told him he hoped to play center field.

Ben scratched his head. "Well, I don't know about that. We had a pretty good center fielder last year. We lost some other guys, though, which is why there are even spots open on the team. One guy who was really good moved away. Guess you'll just have to see what Coach Winston has available."

Sandy nodded, then left. What Ben had said had alarmed him. *But the coach will have to at least let me try,* Sandy thought hopefully. *After all, he doesn't know what I can do!*

Sandy kept his mind off the upcoming Raptors practice by concentrating on the Dolphins team. The kids had played two more games, taking home one win and one loss. They had one more to play before the end of the season, and everyone, including Coach Richards, was hoping to come away with a winning season. So they all agreed to put in an extra practice the Wednesday before the game. Mr. Richards agreed to stop by, too. He said he had something for Sandy.

Sandy was helping Chuck Willoughby practice catching fly balls when Mr. Richards showed up.

"Willoughby, the important thing to remember is to keep your eye on the ball at all times. Watch it drop out of the sky, then nab it!"

Chuck's lower lip stuck out. "I told you, I can't do it!" he said angrily. "Every time a ball comes my way, I drop it. But I don't care. It's just a stupid game, anyway." He pulled his glove off and threw it on the ground.

Sandy bent down, picked up the glove, and dusted it off. "Hey, listen, everyone flubs a play now and then. No one expects you to be perfect. But we do expect you to try." He handed the glove back to the young boy. "So why don't you give it a few more tries, okay?"

Willoughby reluctantly put the glove back on his hand. "Okay," he said. "I'll try again."

"That's my man," Sandy said. He stood up and saw Mr. Richards waving at him. "I gotta go for a minute, but you keep on doing the drill."

Sandy jogged over to Mr. Richards. With a satisfied nod, his probation officer said, "Nice work with that boy."

"Yeah, well, seems he was having an attitude problem. I figured I should try to correct it before he turned out like me." He gave a lopsided smile.

Mr. Richards smiled back. "He could turn out worse," he said. He handed Sandy a packet of papers. "Here, read and sign this. It says you've finished your community service as required. Once this paperwork goes through, the whole incident will be wiped from your record. What do you say to that?"

"I say, where do I sign?"

9

Sandy didn't think anything could have made him any happier than signing those papers. But two days later, he had to stop himself from grinning like an idiot.

The Dolphins had won their last game the night before. Chuck Willoughby himself had made the final out with a good clean catch. Coach Richards and his brother had taken the team for pizza to celebrate. Then, to Sandy's surprise, the kids presented him with a handmade plaque that read, *To Sandy, a Good Coach and a Good Friend, from His Team, the Dolphins.* Beneath it, everyone had signed their names. Sandy had hung it on the wall in his new bedroom.

But now, that moment seemed miles away. It was Friday afternoon. The Raptors were playing a scrimmage game so their coach could check out his players. Sandy stood in center field. The cool green grass was under his cleats, his well-oiled glove was on his hand, and a brand-new Raptors baseball cap was on his head.

Now's my chance to show everyone what I'm made of, he thought with determination. *Clean slate, isn't that what they call it when you start out fresh?*

A high fly ball soared into the air in front of him. He ran in and scooped it up before it hit the grass, then rifled a clean, fast, and right-on-the-mark throw to third base. He'd been doing the same thing all practice. He caught everything that came his way and made sure the others could do the same.

Batting practice started out a little less sure. But the Raptors' coach helped him adjust his stance so that he could get a little more heft into his swing. He missed the first two pitches as he adjusted to the strange new feeling. He belted the third ball high and deep . . . deep . . . yes! It went over the back-field fence.

"Nice, very nice, Sandy," said Coach Winston. "Now we have to work on consistency. You have to be able to deliver on a regular basis. Let's give Pete Phillips a rest. Head out to third base. Get a move on it."

Sandy was startled. *Third base? I'm an outfielder. What's he doing putting me at third? I've never played third before,* he thought. He shot a look to the center field position. Tony Cataldo, a burly fifteen-year-old, stood there, waiting for the next ball. Sandy recalled the coach welcoming Tony warmly at the beginning of practice. *I bet he's the one who played center for the Raptors before. So how am I going to get myself back to that position?*

"Heads up!" shouted the coach. "Let's see some ball playing out there!"

Luckily there wasn't much action at third that inning. Sandy fumbled around but managed not to disgrace himself. His throwing arm came through on a long peg to first base that hit the mark for an out.

But the real excitement was in the outfield. The coach must have told the pitcher to give the hitters something to sink their teeth into. The balls soared from left to right, but especially to center. Sandy watched Tony carefully. The big teen's game seemed a little off. His throws weren't quite as clean as they should be. There was no doubt that he could play the position — Sandy just thought he could play it better than Tony.

When practice ended, the coach had them all seated on the bench for a talk.

"You did well out there," he said. "I think we're in for a good summer. But we're up against a strong team, the Ravens, in our first game. Most of those players are returning from a winning season last year. It's going to take real teamwork to beat them. So come to practice tomorrow and the next day ready to dig in. I'll be figuring out the starting lineup during that time, which means I'll be watching each of you very closely."

When he heard that, Sandy decided to talk to the coach about putting him in center field.

"Uh, Coach Winston?" he called nervously. "I was hoping that in tomorrow's practice you might give me a shot at center field."

The coach looked Sandy up and down. "Tony's my center fielder, Comstock. He played there last year. I don't see any reason to move him around."

"But if you could just give me a chance to —"

The coach shrugged. "I need a third baseman. You've got a good arm, and you seem good at the plate. I might like to start you. Or are you saying you'd rather sub in at center than start at third?"

Sandy swallowed and shook his head. "No, sir. If you think I can be your third baseman, I'll be happy to try."

"Okay, then. Glad we understand each other." The coach turned his back on him and walked to his car.

As Sandy watched him go, a prickle of disappointment crawled up his spine.

He barely gave me a chance to show him what I can do. Some summer this is going to be.

Sandy felt a tap on his shoulder. He spun around to see Ben Eaton standing behind him.

"So, what did you think of practice?" Ben asked.

"Guess I'd be happier if the coach hadn't railroaded me into a position I know nothing about," Sandy muttered.

"Hey, you should feel honored. Coach Winston didn't think he'd find anyone good enough to replace the guy who played third last year."

"Oh, yeah?" Sandy replied. "Who was this superstar?"

"Kid named Perry Warden. I guess you should thank him for having a position at all. If he hadn't moved to Grantville last fall, you'd be out on your can."

Sandy was taken aback by this new information but tried to sound casual. "Yeah, well, if I ever see him, I'll be sure to shake his hand."

Ben picked up his glove and started to walk away. "Oh, I'll bet you'll see him. He's sure to drop by at some point. He's got a lot of friends on the team still."

10

What Sandy had learned from Ben put him in a foul mood for the rest of the day. His disposition hadn't improved by the next day's practice. He played third base with one eye on Tony in center field. Any mistake Tony made only added fuel to his fire.

This guy's not that good, he thought after Tony scrambled to retrieve a dropped ball, then rifled it to the wrong base. *If the coach had given me a chance, I'd have shown everyone I deserved the center field spot. I'd play a real team game.*

"Heads up, Sandy!" called the pitcher, Mitch Lessem, from the mound. Sandy snapped back to attention but missed the hot grounder hit between short and third. He sprinted to pick it up and tossed the ball back to Mitch. The runner made it to second.

As he returned to third, a movement off the field

caught his eye. He glanced over to see what it was — and sucked in his breath.

Hunkered down against the fence was a familiar figure. A figure with red hair. Perry Warden.

"Nice play, Comstock," Perry said mockingly. "Why don't you go back to coaching?"

The heat rose in Sandy's face. But he refused to show that he had heard.

Coach Winston called an end to the day a moment later and walked onto the field to pick up the bases. When he came to third, he spotted the boy near the fence. He broke into a wide grin.

"Hey, Perry! Didn't expect to see you here. Come by to see your old team play?" he called.

Perry stood up and leaned over the fence. "I heard from some of the guys you had some new faces here," he said. He stared over Coach Winston's shoulder at Sandy. "Hope they're not giving you any problems."

The coach shook his head. "So far, no one's given me cause for concern."

"That's good. 'Cause all it takes is one person to ruin things, doesn't it?" Perry agreed. "Just one person."

While the coach and Perry continued to chat, a

few of the other Raptors joined them. Tony Cataldo was among them. Sandy grabbed his glove and hurried off the field. His mind whirled the whole way home.

This is just great, he thought bitterly. *Am I ever going to get a break from that one guy? Everywhere I go, he turns up!*

Then a dark thought struck him. *What if he's telling the coach and those players about what happened?* Memories of how his old Raiders teammates had treated him flooded his brain. So did Mr. Richards's advice to tell the story himself before someone else told for him. *But what can I do? They're his friends — who're they going to believe, him or me? I'm not even sure I want to tell them! If he doesn't, why should I? The less they know, the better, as far as I'm concerned!*

Over and over the same questions and problems flew around his mind. But he couldn't seem to come up with a solution to any of them any more than he could figure out a way to move from third base to center field.

11

During the rest of the week's practices, Sandy kept to himself. He watched his teammates carefully to see if they were treating him any differently. And he scrutinized everything the coach said to him.

By the end of the week, he was almost certain the coach had it in for him. Where he was chummy with the other players, he was gruff with Sandy. He pounded him with instruction about the third base position. He barked at him to correct his batting stance, to be quicker picking up ground balls, and to stop hesitating on his throws.

"You're going to have to do better than that if you're going to be my third baseman," Coach Winston said more than once.

The constant pressure to learn the new position and the thought of Perry Warden showing up again had Sandy's stomach in knots. Even worse, he began to suspect that the other players knew about Perry and him. They suddenly were asking him a lot of questions about what his life had been like in Grantville.

"So when you weren't playing baseball, what did you do for fun?" Mark Freedman, the first baseman, queried after one practice.

Sandy looked at him suspiciously. "The usual stuff, just like anyone."

Another heavyset boy asked if all the convenience stores had candy and soda.

"How would I know?" Sandy answered hotly. He picked up his glove and shoved it into his backpack.

"Grantville's school is so monstrous, I bet you didn't even know everyone in your class," someone else challenged.

"Yeah? Well, I had my group of friends, just like everyone else." Sandy turned his back on his teammates and hurried to his bike. As he was unlocking it, he saw the three boys look at one another. Mark Freedman shook his head and mumbled something to the other two. They glanced at Sandy, then nodded knowingly.

The next day only a few kids asked him any

questions. And in the days that followed, no one asked him anything at all.

To Sandy, their silence spoke volumes. They knew. And there wasn't anything he could do about it.

That Saturday, the Raptors had their first game. They were playing the Ravens, the team Coach Winston had said was one of the best last year, strong in every category. Sandy was slotted to start at third.

The coach's pep talk before the game did little to boost Sandy's enthusiasm for his position. While the other players psyched each other up, he sat silently in the stands, waiting for the game to begin.

In the first inning, the Ravens proved that they deserved their reputation. They led off by putting four men on base and scoring one run on a bunt before Mitch retired the side. Sandy managed to put away one sizzling drive that practically tore a hole in his glove.

Sandy was third in the batting order. If either of the first two Raptors batters could get on base, he stood a chance of driving in the first run. That would make the coach sit up and pay attention. Of course, if the first two batters made outs, Sandy was in line for ending the inning if he failed to get a solid hit. It was a win-or-lose situation.

Well, I'm going to win, whether they care or not, he thought as he swung two bats to warm up.

"Come on, Raptors! Beat those Ravens!" called their fans from the stands.

Mark Freedman, first baseman for the Raptors, tilted his batting cap, then squinted at the pitcher. The pitcher stared back and threw the first pitch. Mark swung at it and missed.

He missed the next two, too. One out for the Raptors.

Second baseman Frank Maxwell did better. He waited it out and took a walk on the sixth pitch.

Then it was Sandy's turn. He put down one bat and headed with the other for the plate. Just before he got there, he glanced toward the runner on first. As he did so, his eyes picked up a familiar thatch of red hair.

Perry Warden was sitting in the stands, as cool as a cucumber. He was staring right at Sandy.

Sandy's step faltered.

"You gonna stand there all day or are you gonna play ball?" the Ravens' catcher shouted to him.

With a start, Sandy stepped into the batter's box.

He lowered the brim of his batting helmet and tried to concentrate on the game. But he couldn't. The first pitch came right down the middle for a called strike.

He came around in time to swing at the next pitch. He missed it for the second strike against him.

He stepped out of the box to give himself time to collect his thoughts. But his mind was a jumble. When he swung at the next pitch, he tipped the ball for a pop-up toward first. It was easily put away for the second out.

"I guess my batting lessons were wasted," said the coach when Sandy got back to the dugout.

Sandy suddenly remembered Coach Winston's advice on correcting his stance.

"Sorry, Coach, it just slipped my mind," Sandy mumbled. But the coach was already focusing on the next batter.

Left fielder Philip Wood made the third out, sending the Raptors back onto the field.

Sandy grabbed his glove and started out toward third base. He carefully avoided looking at the stands but felt Perry Warden's stare all the same.

What is it with that guy? he thought. *Why does he have to keep hounding me?*

No matter how hard he tried, Sandy just couldn't put Perry Warden out of his thoughts. In the third inning, a fly ball came sailing in his direction. Sandy should have put it away easily. Instead he was staring at the dirt between his toes, miles away in thought.

Luckily, the roar of the crowd woke him up and he managed to make the catch. But he was off stride, and his peg to first went wide. Runners advanced from first and second to second and third. With the Raptors down 2–0 and only one out, the Ravens had a chance for a real breakaway.

Coach Winston shook his head on the sidelines. "Come on, Comstock! Let's keep your mind on the game!"

"Yeah, Sandy, that should have been an easy out," the Raptors' shortstop hissed at him. "Our third baseman last year could have done that play in his sleep."

Sandy jabbed the dirt angrily. *Why don't you just come right out and say you wish he was here instead of me? I know you're thinking it, and so does everyone else!*

Mitch finally ended the half-inning by putting the next two batters away without incident. It was midway through the game. If the Raptors were to win it, they had to come alive.

"What's wrong with you guys?" asked the coach, stalking up and down in front of the bench. "Wake up! Let's play some baseball out there! Let's hear some chatter at least! Jimmy, get up there and show us your stuff."

Jimmy Dobson wasn't a long ball hitter, but he hit them hard. Now, in the bottom of the third, he was the leadoff batter for the Raptors. Their hopes were centered on him for the moment.

"Come on, Jimmy! You can do it!"

Jimmy did do it. He smashed a line drive that sizzled by the pitcher. It practically skimmed the top off second base before slashing through the turf into center field. It was one of those low hits that can be scooped up if the timing is right.

But the Ravens' center fielder was off the mark. By the time the ball made it to the third baseman's mitt, Jimmy was dusting off his pants and grinning.

"That guy should have been moving toward the ball way before he did," Sandy remarked to no one in particular. "I've fielded tons of those hits without a problem by doing that. Anyone who plays center field should know how to pick those up."

Sandy felt a pair of eyes on him. Tony Cataldo was staring at him.

"What do you mean, you've fielded tons of those?" Tony asked. His tone was anything but friendly.

"I used to play center field," Sandy replied.

"Oh, yeah? Were you any better there than you are at third?"

"I was a lot better than some people I know!" Sandy retorted.

"What's that supposed to mean?" Tony asked angrily.

Coach Winston cut in. "Knock it off, you two. Pay attention to the game."

Tony stood up and headed for the water jug after giving Sandy a nasty look. Sandy pretended he didn't see it. Instead, he focused on the plate. He was just in time to see Mitch Lessem strike out.

Now the top of the batting order was up. It wouldn't take much to send Jimmy home. Mark hadn't gotten a clean hit yet and was out to redeem himself. He worked the count up to 2 and 2, then proceeded to pop off five foul balls in a row — all of them to the left. If Jimmy didn't pay attention, a caught ball could turn into an easy double play. Mark woofed the next pitch to strike out, so the runner remained on third.

Now it was Frank's turn to bring it all home. He had walked on his first at bat but singled his next two times. He was a definite threat.

The Ravens figured that out, too. The pitcher walked the second baseman again.

With two men on base and two outs, Sandy strode to the plate.

The Ravens' coach called for a time-out. Coach Winston took the time to talk to Sandy.

"A hit now could mean the difference in the

game," he said, cocking an eyebrow at Sandy. "So try to remember about the new stance this time."

"Yes, Coach," said Sandy tightly. He hitched up his pants, tightened his batting glove, and headed for the plate.

Sandy had a good feel for how the Ravens' pitcher played the game. He guessed that his first pitch would be down the middle but would break to the inside, causing the batter to back off a little. If he wanted to take a chance on swinging at it, the smart thing to do would be to back off the minute the pitch was thrown. That's what some of the guys had started doing.

But Sandy decided that he'd be off balance enough to lose any control over where he hit the ball. Better to wait it out.

The pitch came and nearly brushed against Sandy's waistline. He had guessed right. Ball one.

If the pitcher stayed true to his routine, the next pitch would be a little higher and slightly outside. That was the kind Sandy really liked.

But it was too high and too outside. Ball two.

The Ravens crowd roared its disapproval. Was

their pitcher going to walk Sandy and load the bases?

Sandy knew that he should wait the next pitch out. He was ahead of the pitcher and had little to lose.

The ball zoomed down the middle for a called strike. The count was now 2 and 1. Sandy thought he knew what to expect. The ball would probably head for the lowest point of the strike zone, and then sink. To hit it, he'd have to swing the bat in a scooping stroke. But if he caught it right, well, good things would happen.

The ball came exactly as Sandy had expected. If it had broken any lower, he'd have had to hit the plate before he made contact with it. But he found his mark.

Crack!

Ash wood connected with the white sphere and sent it rocketing high over the field, deep, deep, deep toward center field — and over the fence!

Sandy jogged around the field to thunderous cheers from the stands. A cluster of Raptors waiting outside the dugout slapped him high fives. But only one player congratulated him.

"Great hit, Sandy!" Ben Eaton enthused. "From the looks of that swing, you'd make a good golfer if you ever gave up baseball!"

Sandy smiled at him, started toward the bench, then stopped abruptly. The spot he usually took was occupied.

By Perry Warden.

Sandy immediately turned away and took another seat farther down the bench. But the redhead slid down until he was next to him.

"Nice hit, Comstock. You must have learned something from the sports magazine you 'borrowed' once, huh?"

Sandy tried his best to ignore him. But Ben Eaton interfered.

"Hey, Perry, you know Sandy?" Ben asked curiously.

"You mean Sandy hasn't told about how we met in Grantville?"

Sandy shifted his eyes to Ben, then to Perry. "No," he said simply.

"How did you meet?" Ben asked. Perry stared at Sandy for a moment, then gave a half smile.

"Never mind" was all Perry said. He stood up,

stretched, said hello and slapped high fives with a few other players, then left.

There were two more innings to play, but for Sandy, the excitement was gone. In its place was confusion. He spent the rest of the game at third base but played only halfheartedly.

The Raptors took the win, thanks to Sandy's three-run homer. If it had been any other team, Sandy would have been shouting victoriously. But his mind was still on the conversation on the bench.

He wasn't sure, but Perry had seemed to be fishing around to see how much Ben knew about Sandy and him. That could only mean that Perry hadn't said a word about the past trouble to Ben.

And if he hasn't told Ben, maybe he hasn't said anything to anyone else, either. But if that's true, why does everyone except Ben treat me like I've got the plague?

13

Sandy spent most of Sunday in his room. On Monday, it was raining too hard for practice to be held. But Tuesday dawned clear and sunny. And that was the day Sandy decided to get to the bottom of the mystery of the Raptors.

During the warm-up, Sandy took a quick look around to see if a certain redhead had appeared again. He hadn't. When the warm-up was over, Sandy took a seat next to Ben Eaton.

While the coach called out the starting lineup for a scrimmage, Sandy nonchalantly said, "So, it was weird that Perry Warden was here for the game, wasn't it?"

Ben shrugged. "He likes baseball, and he was one of our star players last year. Guess he just wanted to come back and see how we were doing." He turned his attention back to the coach.

"Is he the guy who moved away last year?" Sandy prodded.

Ben glanced at him and nodded. "He's been living in Grantville ever since his parents divorced last spring. I don't think he gets back here that often."

"You sound like you know him pretty well," Sandy said, hoping Ben would keep talking.

"I know he's a good ballplayer. But when his parents were going through the divorce, I think he was kind of messed up. Turned mean." Ben turned to face Sandy completely. "Why are you so interested in him, anyway?"

"No reason," Sandy said hastily. "Hey, I think practice is about to begin."

Later on, Sandy joined Frank Maxwell in the on-deck circle.

"So, how about that Perry Warden, coming by to cheer for the team on Saturday?" he said.

Frank grunted.

"Guess you guys miss having him on the team."

Frank shrugged. "He was a good third baseman," he muttered.

Sandy tried again. "You ever hear anything about what he's been up to in Grantville?"

Frank eyeballed him. "He said he was coaching some kids' team this summer. That, and doing some stuff for the town." He stood up and walked to the plate, leaving Sandy behind to wonder if Frank knew what "some stuff for the town" meant. Sandy suspected that it was Perry's way of covering up his probation work.

Still later during that practice, Sandy cornered Mitch Lessem by the water jug. "You know, it's too bad Perry Warden moved away. I hear he would have been a real asset to the team."

Mitch looked at Sandy over the cup of water he was drinking. "I'm sure if Perry's on a ball team in Grantville, he's giving it his all, just like he did here."

"You mean you don't know if he's playing for a team or not?"

"He dropped out of sight once he moved away. I was kind of surprised to see him at our game the other day, as a matter of fact. I couldn't figure out what he was doing here. Trying to relive last year's glories, maybe."

By the end of practice, Sandy felt he had the

answer to one important question: Perry Warden had not told his old teammates about the trouble he'd been in. Yet to his surprise, the relief he felt was tinged with anxiety still.

The reason was suddenly obvious to him: Even though Perry hadn't said anything yet, that didn't mean he never would. And since it seemed the team had for some reason decided to turn against Sandy, the likelihood was great that they'd believe whatever Perry had to say.

Sandy was living on borrowed time. Unless he could figure out why his teammates didn't like him, the clock might run out at any time. But he couldn't do that without help.

14

When Sandy got home that night, he rushed to his room and dug through his top desk drawer. At last, he pulled a slip of paper out from the pile of junk. On it was a phone number and a name.

Cradling the phone to his shoulder, Sandy dialed. Someone picked up after the first ring.

"Hello?"

"Coach Richards? This is Sandy Comstock."

"Sandy! Good to hear from you. How's the New-town summer league going?" Coach Richards's friendly voice put Sandy at ease instantly.

"Actually, Coach, that's why I'm calling. Have you got a minute?"

"Shoot," said Coach Richards.

For the next ten minutes, Sandy spoke nonstop. He told the coach everything he could remember about the Raptors' season from the beginning. He left out nothing: the coach's refusal to let him play center field, the players' curious questions about Grantville, Perry Warden's sudden appearances, and his faltering play at third base.

"I just can't seem to make my way with this team, Coach," he finished at last.

Coach Richards blew out his breath in a big huff. "Okay, Sandy, I'll tell you how I see it. This Perry Warden fellow isn't the only one working against you."

Sandy was startled. "He isn't? Who's the other guy? Do I know him?"

Coach Richards chuckled. "Yes, you know him. You see him every time you look in a mirror."

"*Me?* What do you mean — that *I'm* the reason no one likes me? But I never did or said anything to anyone!"

"Listen to what you just said, Sandy. From what you've told me, you've done exactly nothing to get to know your teammates. You've been so busy trying to analyze everything they say and to cover up anything about your dark past, that you've wound up alienating yourself from them! Friendship is a two-way street, don't forget. You've got to be open with them if you expect them to be the same with you. Remember how your positive attitude helped the Dolphins improve!"

Sandy thought that over. "But how can I be open with them and not tell them about my — my dark past?"

"Why do you want to keep that from them? Everyone makes mistakes, Sandy. Sure, yours was a little worse than others, but you paid the price. With interest, as far as I'm concerned. And I'm sure my brother has warned you of the dangers of letting others tell your story for you. There's nothing harder to squash than a rumor gone wild."

Sandy was unconvinced and told him so.

"Well, you could try starting with something simpler, I guess. Like winning them over with your spectacular play on the field and showing enthusiasm for your team. I know you can do that."

Sandy hung up with that advice in his head. He decided it was the best place to start, for now.

How he was going to go about winning over his teammates was the question brewing in his mind the next day at practice and the one that followed that. In fact, he was so preoccupied with his thoughts that he started to play poorly on the field. By the end of the second day, Coach Winston took him aside.

"Sandy, I don't know what's going on with you, but I'm not having someone with his head in the clouds starting at third base. Tomorrow's game, Josh Grant is my third baseman."

Sandy couldn't believe it. It was the worst thing that could have happened!

The next day, the Raptors hit the field to play the Pelicans.

"Everybody up!" the coach called. The bench came to its feet as both teams and the crowd stood to listen to a tape recording of the "Star-Spangled Banner." Usually that gave Sandy a little flutter of excitement. Today, he scarcely heard the shouts that echoed out around him at the end of the national anthem.

Encouragement rang from the stands as the game began. The Raptors were first up at bat. Mark Freedman was the leadoff batter, with Frank Maxwell on deck. Third up was Josh Grant.

The Pelicans' pitcher was cold starting off. He pitched three consecutive balls, and it looked as though Mark would stroll down to first base. But the next two were rockets down the middle to bring things to a full count.

Mark managed to get a piece of wood into the next pitch. The ball rose high into left field but not deep enough to cause trouble. It was easily put away for out number one.

Any idea that the Pelicans were going to be a pushover quickly vanished.

Frank kept his eye on the ball but watched the count go to 2 and 2. Then he took the next pitch and wiffed it for strike number three.

Josh Grant swung at the first pitch across the plate. The ball curved around the third base line and looked as though it was heading for foul territory. But then it ended its arc and continued to soar over the turf into left field, as close to the foul line as it could go. The Pelican left fielder caught it in his outstretched glove. A fat goose egg went up on the scoreboard for the top of the first inning.

The Pelicans didn't show themselves to be much more at bat than the Raptors had been. Lenny

Burton, a southpaw, was on the mound for the Raptors. His very first pitch was a sizzler that told everyone he meant business.

After striking out the first two batters, he allowed a single to short to put a hit, the first one, on the scoreboard.

But the next Pelican batter hit a high foul ball that hovered above the first base line. Lenny dashed in for it and put it away to end the inning.

Philip Wood was the leadoff batter for the Raptors in the second inning. He carefully selected his bat and started toward the plate.

Cheers rose up from the rest of the team. This time, Sandy added his own.

"Come on, Philip! You can do it!"

Philip managed to hit a line drive beyond the pitcher for a clean, stand-up single. The Raptors were on the scoreboard with their first hit.

It was Jimmy's turn to see what he could do. The count rose to 3 and 2. Jimmy had to look sharp on the next pitch.

When it came, he swung forward with enough power to send the ball soaring toward the wall. But instead of going over for a homer, the ball landed in the mitt of the Pelicans' center fielder.

The next batter, Tony Cataldo, stepped up to the plate. Sandy sat in silence. Tony was a good enough hitter, but Sandy had a feeling his own stats were better.

Tony swung on a breaking pitch and caught it a little inside. The ball flew out to the second baseman, who put it away. He went after Philip, who was making a break for second. Luckily, Philip was fast enough to get there on a slide. His fingers touched the bag a fraction of a second before he was tagged.

The Raptors' hopes for a score were still alive as their shortstop, Dewey Williams, took his chance at the plate. Unfortunately, after popping a foul ball off the third base line, he swung at two bad pitches and the top of the second inning was over.

Lenny let two Pelicans get on base at the bottom of the second. But he managed to hold them there as the next three batters were put away to end a scoreless inning.

In the third inning, a walk put Lenny on base. Ben Eaton, the catcher, sent him home with a stand-up double, and the Raptors were first to draw blood. Unfortunately, they couldn't extend the streak and retired with only one run on the scoreboard.

They held their lead until the bottom of the fifth. Sandy had just about worn out the seat of his pants shifting around on the bench. He had sat out during games before, but never the whole game. The coach seemed satisfied with the lineup, however, even though the Raptors' lead was so thin.

Lenny was tiring. He walked the first two Pelicans before putting out the third batter with some pitches that barely made it into the zone. Finally, Coach Winston called time and walked out to the mound. Ben Eaton and Josh Grant joined him to speak to the southpaw hurler. Sandy figured they were discussing how to handle things if the next batter got a hit. But the talk went on for a longer time than such a discussion needed.

For a moment, it looked like the coach might call in a replacement. But Lenny stayed on the mound as the others returned to their positions.

There was a murmur of excitement as play resumed.

The Pelicans' shortstop was at bat. He shuffled his feet, settled the bat in position, and waited.

Lenny stared down the line. He wound up, hesitated for a second, and then threw.

The ball came zooming along and, like magnet to metal, it connected with the bat.

Craaaack!

The horsehide sphere rose high overhead and sailed over the field deeper and deeper. Finally, it dropped over the fence for a home run. Three Pelican runners crossed the plate to turn the score to their advantage, 3–1.

15

Coach Winston pulled Lenny off the mound and sent in right-hander Mitch Lessem to turn things around. Sandy wondered if any more substitutions were in the offing. If so, where would he end up?

Right where he was seated was the answer. The coach left the rest of the lineup on the field just as it was.

Mitch brought about groans when he walked his first batter. But he gave the fans something to cheer about when he put the next Pelican away one-two-three. He capped the inning by pitching a low ball that the next batter scooped for a pop-up to third base.

The Raptors had one last chance to take the game back for a win. Down by two runs, the lead-off Raptor at the plate was Jimmy.

Jimmy looked as though he was real hungry to help. He did more than that. After waiting out two called strikes and one ball, he swung and connected.

Crack!

The ball went flying high into the sky and then over the fence for a home run! The Raptors were now only one run behind.

After filling the air with cheers, the fans settled down to see what would happen next. With a little bit of luck, the Raptors could tie up the game and even go ahead. The question was: Would Jimmy's homer start a genuine rally? Or would it fizzle with the next batter — Tony Cataldo?

"Come on, you Raptors!"

"Get tough, Raptors!"

"Show us your stuff, Cataldo!"

Tony seemed to have trouble finding his mark on the bat. He bobbled off three foul balls before getting his teeth into the next pitch. The crack of his bat sent the ball out between center and left field about ten yards beyond the baseline. The Pelican outfield scrambled for it, but the ball bounded oddly in the grass. Tony managed to stretch the hit to a double before the Pelicans had things back under control.

With a runner on second and no outs, the Raptors fans were cheering louder than ever.

Dewey Williams had walked once and reached base once on a fielder's choice. Sandy guessed how he felt — ready to get a hit. But maybe he was too ready. Dewey swung at two pitches and watched a third go by for a called strike and the Raptors' first out.

It was now up to Mitch to move things along. But Coach Winston wasn't about to take a chance on Mitch. He looked over the bench and signaled Eddie Sumner, the number-one substitute, to go to the plate. Then he called over to Sandy.

"Comstock, stretch your legs. Get some exercise. You might be needed out there."

Sandy was so surprised that he didn't respond at first. Only when a few members of the team turned to look at him did he follow the coach's instructions. He picked up two bats and practiced his swing.

Silence blanketed the playing field as the Pelicans' pitcher fired the ball down the line to Eddie. It went wide of the mark, so wide that there was no question what was happening. Eddie was being given a deliberate walk. That would bring Ben Eaton up to the plate. Ben had popped out twice this game. With Eddie on first and Tony at third, that increased the chances of tagging someone out to squash the Raptors' chances of winning.

Watching from the dugout, Sandy realized that the Pelicans' coach had made a smart move.

Except for one thing: Ben Eaton was not being sent up to bat. The coach called Sandy over and said to him, "It's up to you, Sandy. This pitcher is familiar with Ben. He knows exactly where his weaknesses are. You might stand a chance of throwing him off."

"I'll give it a try, Coach," said Sandy. Millions of butterflies danced around inside of him.

"Don't try to kill the ball. Take your time, and place it in short right or left field. Take your time."

As Sandy walked to the plate, he felt every eye in the park staring at him. He found his position, tapped his bat on the plate, adjusted his helmet, and stared down the pitcher.

The ball came toward that sweet pocket of space a little below his waist and just so far in front of him. He shifted his weight, lifted his foot, lowered the bat, and slammed into the ball.

Slunk!

His bat barely made contact with the bottom of the horsehide sphere. It rose up in the air about twenty feet, just a yard or so in front of the plate. The Pelicans' catcher reached out and caught it in the center of his mitt for the third and final out — and the end of a losing game for the Raptors.

Sandy just stood there, frozen with despair.

16

The cheers of the Pelicans team lingered in Sandy's ears as he dragged his way back to the bench. None of the Raptors looked at him.

Sandy hurried off the field, stopping only to step into the restroom. When he emerged, a familiar voice called out to him.

"So, baseball boy, I understand you've been asking a lot of questions about me. What gives?" Perry Warden was standing in front of him. He looked angry. "What do you expect to find out?"

Sandy just wasn't in the mood to play games. Mr. Richards, his probation officer, had once told him to deal with a situation head-on. And his brother had only the night before advised him to consider the wisdom of telling his story before someone else did. Well, now that someone was standing in front of him. In the second it took him to fold his arms across his chest, Sandy made up his mind to stop being bullied by Perry Warden's threats.

"Let me ask *you* something. What did *you* expect to find out the other day when you were nosing around the bench?"

Perry looked surprised, but he recovered quickly. "I was just visiting some old friends, that's all."

"Is that a fact? I think you were trying to find out exactly what I found out the other day — whether anyone had heard of the trouble we were in in Grantville," Sandy replied.

Perry reddened. But after a moment, a crafty look crossed his face. "Just because I haven't said anything yet doesn't mean I won't. Once they find out about you, they're not going to want you on the team anymore," he said.

Sandy narrowed his eyes. "And what if I decide to tell them myself? The whole story, that is, not something you make up as you go along." By the look on Perry's face, Sandy knew he had scored a point. He pressed on. "To them, you're still the star of last year's season! How are you going to feel when they find out their shining boy is tarnished?"

Perry sputtered but didn't answer him. After a moment, he spun on his heels and stalked away.

Sandy watched him go. Although he had started it, he was stunned at what had just happened.

I made him squirm, he said to himself. *But where does it leave me? I practically promised I was going to tell! How can I keep quiet now?*

The answer was clear. He couldn't. Because he had backed Perry Warden into a corner and the only way Perry was going to get out was to tell his own story.

And Sandy had a feeling that story wasn't going to paint him in a very nice way. If he was going to salvage anything of his reputation, he had to act fast.

There was just one obstacle to be overcome: Sandy still had to prove to the Raptors that he was worth listening to.

He knew of only one way he could do that for sure. And it wasn't by playing third base, sitting on the bench, or hitting pop-up foul balls.

He had to get back into center field, where he belonged!

17

All weekend long, Sandy tried to come up with an argument that would convince Coach Winston to try him at center field again. But nothing he thought of seemed likely to work.

Then the coach himself provided the opening. At the start of the first Raptors' practice the following week, he called the team together at the bench and delivered a little pep talk.

"I think one of the reasons the team didn't do better last week against the Pelicans is a lack of teamwork. Everyone is taking it for granted that the other guy will do it. You've become a little too settled in your slots. So this week, I'm going to shift you around. You'll see what it's like to play the other guy's position, and maybe you'll think a little more about what you do out there," he said. "Now, take fifteen minutes to warm up and come back when I whistle. We'll have a little practice game just to see what happens."

When the whistle blew a quarter of an hour later, every member of the team was curious to see where he'd be playing. Although none of them had any idea, Sandy was a little more anxious than the others. Not only did he not know what position, he wasn't even sure he'd be on any roster — after what had happened to end the Pelicans game.

The coach finished the first team, then went on to the second. Sandy was right at the top of the list — at center field!

When the game began, Sandy didn't have much to do. Tony Cataldo, of all people, was on the pitcher's mound. He walked the first three batters until he found the strike zone. Then the fourth went down swinging, and the fifth hit into a double play.

Sandy was slated to bat in the fifth position, so he figured he probably wouldn't be up that inning. But the pitcher for the opposing team was Jimmy. Surprisingly, he knew a thing or two about putting the ball across the plate. He let the first batter reach first on a single that just went by the second baseman, and then put the next two batters away with strikeouts.

"Hey, pitcher man!"

"Looks like mound material to me, Coach!"

The good-natured cries rang out as Sandy moved toward the plate. And then, suddenly, they quieted down. There was little cheering as he settled into the batter's box.

Only the voice of Coach Winston could be heard shouting over to him, "Give that new stance a try again, Sandy." It made the silence of the rest of the team more noticeable.

Sandy took a deep breath. Breaking the ice with his teammates after three weeks was going to be tougher than he thought. But he called back an "okay" to the coach and struck the new stance.

Unfortunately, Jimmy wasn't giving him much to hit. He fouled one to the first base stand and one to the third base side of the park. Then he saw a pitch he liked. He swung with all his might.

Crack!

The ball soared high into right field. Mitch Lessem scrambled in for the catch. But suddenly, a second white object flashed in the sky. It was another base-ball, hit into the field by a group of people playing a pickup game!

A split second after Sandy's ball hit the ground, the second ball landed a few feet away. Mitch ran toward one ball. Ben Eaton, the center fielder, ran to the other. Intent on making the play, they didn't see each other until they had fielded the ball and were about ready to throw. Then they caught sight of each other. Both hesitated in mid-heave, then continued their throws. The second baseman just ducked out of the way.

Sandy couldn't help it. As he rounded second base, he started to chuckle. By the time he reached home, he could barely move he was laughing so hard.

"That was the lamest home run I've ever hit!" he gasped. "Coach, how are you going to rule that one? A two-run homer, or an attempted double play?"

The other players stared at him. Then Ben Eaton started laughing, too. Others joined in. Even Coach Winston grinned.

For the rest of the practice, the players talked

about the incident, changing the story until it had grown in absurdity.

"Sandy had a ball tucked up his sleeve. What happened was, he thought he struck out. Didn't even realize he'd hit it, he was so busy digging that ball out from his sleeve and heaving it into center field."

"No, what happened was, Jimmy fired his pitches down so quickly that Sandy hit the first ball with a regular swing, the second one when he was pulling the bat back into position!"

"You're all wrong! You know how Sandy likes to take warm-up swings with two bats? Well, Jimmy decided he'd send down two balls for him to hit with his two bats. Sandy hit the one as he tossed away the first bat, the second with the bat he was still holding!"

Sandy laughed along with the rest. For the first time since he'd become a Raptor, he felt like part of the team.

At the end of practice, Coach Winston called them all together. "Tomorrow, I'll have most of you back playing your old spots. Some of you may find yourself in new positions. And some," he added with a smile, "may find yourself cooling your heels until you shape up and stop all this horsing around!"

As Sandy left practice, he heard something he hadn't heard for a long time. It was the sound of his teammates calling out good-byes to him and promises to see him at practice the next day.

The next day's practice started out with a number of routine drills. But it also featured a practice game between two squads the coach had put together.

Sandy waited eagerly to hear his name called. When it was, he couldn't help but grin. "Sandy Comstock, center field — second string."

Okay, here we go, Comstock, he said to himself. *Here's your big chance to show the coach who his first starting center fielder should be. Tony's an okay guy, but you're the better player.*

Sandy played his hardest that game. He dove and jumped for balls, threw hard and accurately, took his time at the plate, and kept up a constant stream of encouraging chatter. And the other players of the second string responded. For the first time since the beginning of the season, the starting squad lost the scrimmage.

The next three days, he stayed in the center field position for the second string. But on Friday, when Coach Winston called out the roster of starters, Tony Cataldo had been moved to third base — and Sandy Comstock was named for center field.

Coach Winston took both boys aside before the scrimmage. "Listen, Tony, I'm going with Sandy out there because he's really shown me something this week. He's played some stellar ball, and he's earned a chance. And I want to see what you can do in the infield."

Sandy braced himself for a protest.

Tony nodded. "Okay, Coach. Whatever's best for the team. Sandy seems to know what he's doing out there. And I wouldn't mind a change," he said simply. And that was that.

Sandy was so psyched to be back in his spot that he almost decided not to follow through on telling his teammates about his trouble in Grantville. But one day, Perry Warden showed up at the end of practice, and Sandy's old anxieties came rushing back. Although Perry stuck around for only a few minutes and avoided him the entire time, Sandy knew he could no longer take a chance with him.

Sandy's opportunity to tell his story came the following week. It wasn't the way he would have chosen, however. During a practice game that Wednesday, Ben went chasing a wild pitch that flew near the back stand. He was so intent on the ball that he didn't see the pole. Two seconds later, he was lying dazed on the ground. The coach called a time-out. Since Sandy was waiting to bat, he helped the coach get Ben to the bench.

Ben lay down while the coach pressed an ice pack to his forehead.

"Ooh, that's cold," Ben mumbled. "Boy, do I feel dumb. Bet you've never made a stupid mistake like that before."

Sandy chuckled. "Well, maybe not on the ball field. But I've made some stupid mistakes in my time. Once I made a *really* stupid mistake."

Ben shifted slightly and looked up at his teammate. "Oh, yeah? What was it? Come on, make a dying man feel better."

Sandy took a deep breath. He started out slow,

faltering a little as the story spun out and not looking at Ben as he told it. But by the time he reached the part about serving probation, Ben was sitting up and listening intently. When he had finished, Ben whistled.

"Man, I thought I sensed some tension between you and Perry," he said. "But I never would have guessed that. I just figured he was jealous because you were in his old spot on the team." He was silent for a moment, then turned and looked at Sandy.

"Listen, Sandy, I appreciate your telling me this. Not because I wanted to know all your deep, dark secrets. Remember how I told you once that Perry had turned kind of mean last year? You found out about that firsthand, I guess, but I really want you to know that he wasn't always like that. I think everything just kind of got to him all at once: his parents' divorce, having to move right after being a star on the team, leaving all his friends behind, that kind of thing. And I don't think he'd ever admit it, but I'm pretty sure the idea of moving from small-town Newtown to big-city Grantville scared him. So he just kind of took on this tough-guy image, you know?"

Sandy was silent. He thought about how he had been before moving to Newtown: angry, defiant, and mad at his parents all the time. It was as though he and Perry had switched places in the past year. He wondered if Perry felt the same way. If he did, Sandy guessed that seeing him in the third base slot had been the last straw.

But understanding the guy didn't make Sandy feel much better about him. He knew they'd never be buddies — but so long as they weren't enemies, he'd take it. He knew he'd do his part to make that happen.

Over the next few days, Sandy's story made its way around the team. To his relief, he found that most of the players were interested in what had happened, but not terribly judgmental. Sandy wondered if they understood because they had had some of their own scrapes and troubles.

Whatever the truth was, Sandy was just glad that he had told his own story. Because now that he had, he could focus on the really important things — like winning baseball games!

From that moment on, Sandy never let his focus

drift. He concentrated on doing his best, and it showed. His fielding was up to its old Raider standard, and his hitting got better each time he came up to bat. There was no question that he was a better center fielder than Tony. But since Tony proved to be a better third baseman than Sandy, everyone came out on top.

19

The day of the last summer league game arrived. It was a bright August afternoon, and the Raptors were preparing to defend their first-place position against the number-two team, the Hawks.

The Hawks had first ups.

Pitching for the Raptors was Mitch Lessem. He kept the action in the infield and gave up only one hit before retiring the side.

The Raptors didn't do that well when their turn came. Mark struck out, Frank hit one straight into the waiting glove of the Hawks' shortstop, and Tony bobbled one down to first but couldn't outrun the peg.

Mitch held the Hawks hitless at the top of the second, giving up his first walk of the game but fanning two batters in a row. Still, the outfield hadn't seen much action.

Sandy led off for the Raptors at the bottom of the second inning. As he walked toward the plate, he paid a lot more attention to the sounds that followed him from the dugout. Those were his teammates shouting encouragement.

"Go, you Raptor!"

"Come on, Sandy, you can do it!"

"Eye on the ball, champ!"

Over toward third base, he saw a familiar face in the stands: Perry Warden. But instead of letting that spook him, Sandy just smiled. He cared more about his team. He knew he had to do his best for them. He could do that only by concentrating on everything he had learned from every coach who had helped him with his batting.

First he waited for the release before really focusing on the ball. He made sure he was balanced, with his feet spread wide apart. He relaxed his muscles, particularly his grip on the bat, not trying to squeeze it to death. Then, as the ball came his way, he shifted his weight to his back leg and turned his front shoulder inward. When he decided to go for it, he moved his weight forward, with his front leg slightly bent. At the moment of contact, he locked his front leg and let his back leg and hip explode toward the ball. His front arm was fully extended, his back arm and hand remained behind the bat.

Craaaack!

The ball went soaring into the sky, curving slightly toward left field. It reached the top of its arc somewhere in midfield before it began to drop — behind the fence.

Home run!

Sandy had come through to launch the Raptors on their way. He rounded the bases, head down and arms churning. As he crossed home plate, he was instantly surrounded by teammates slapping high fives on him and hugging him as hard as they could.

But the game was far from over. In the next two innings, Mitch loosened his iron grip. The top of the Hawks' batting order torched the Raptors pitcher for two runs that put the Hawks ahead 2–1.

In his second time at bat, Sandy had waited out the pitcher and walked after a full count. But no one had been able to send him home. As he came to bat in the fifth inning, he was anxious to fire things up for the Raptors. Frank had managed to hit one deep into right field and outrace the peg to second for a double. He was a fast runner and might score if Sandy could give him something to travel on. Sandy decided he would try to give him his ticket.

After waiting out two low and outside pitches, he picked a high ball that started to drop as it neared the plate. He swung with all his might and smoked a liner that popped in and out of the Hawks' second baseman's glove. Frank took off like a speeding bullet and beat the throw home. Sandy had chalked up a game-tying single.

The score was now tied at 2–2. The rally had begun, and Philip Wood kept things going with a two-bagger that sent Sandy to third base. There was only one out on the scoreboard when Jimmy Dobson stepped up to the plate. He went for a sacrifice. It worked. Sandy beat the peg to home, while Philip crossed to second and slid into third. Once again, Sandy was swarmed by his teammates.

Dewey Williams was fanned for the third and final out, and the Raptors took to the field with a one-run lead at the top of the sixth and final inning.

The top of the Hawks' batting order came up to the plate. Inspired by the previous inning's rally, Mitch recovered his control. He gave up one hit to their leadoff batter but held the next one in check with a strikeout. Then the third Hawk pounded Mitch for a single. Players at first and second, and only one out.

The Hawks' cleanup batter, their left fielder, was their leading hitter. He had a reputation for hitting the short ball just over the second baseman's head.

"Let's play in, guys!" Sandy called to the left and right fielders. They all jogged in another ten feet for good measure.

But Sandy kept himself flexible — just in case. His instincts proved to be on target.

The Hawks' batter took a mighty swing and turned out a high fly ball toward center. At first, it didn't seem like it would go the distance. But it did. Instead of dropping into the sweet spot behind second, it continued arcing upward, heading straight for the fence.

Sandy dashed back, following it with his eyes. The ball descended like a rocket just inside the fence.

Sandy lunged into the air, stretched out his glove —
and caught it!

But even as he was squeezing the ball into the
webbing, he knew that the runners on first and second weren't standing still. They were going to try to
make it for home. If one of them did, the game
would be tied at 3–3. If both did, well, the Raptors
might just kiss this victory good-bye, unless they
could score two runs at the bottom of the sixth. But
if he could help stop *both* runners . . .

The moment his feet touched the ground, Sandy
spun around, locked one foot in a pivot, and pegged
the ball to Tony at third.

Smack! The ball was trapped in the cup of Tony's
outstretched glove. He reached out and tagged the
runner. Out!

The cheers rang out from the stands and the Raptors bench. As Sandy ran in from the outfield, he
was mobbed first by the left and right fielders, then
the infield. The last guy to reach him was Ben
Eaton.

Ben slapped him on the back, grinning ear to ear.
"What a play!" he cried. "Is this really the same

guy who walked around at the start of the season with a chip on his shoulder the size of Rhode Island?"

"That's what we wondered," a familiar voice said.

Sandy looked through the crowd of Raptors and spied Mr. Richards and his brother. He tried to break free from his teammates and go speak to them, but the Raptors had other ideas. They hoisted their center fielder to their shoulders and started to parade him around the bases.

As Sandy was jostled about, he looked over his shoulder back at the two brothers. They were smiling widely. Coach Richards gave him a thumbs-up, then they both waved, turned, and headed for the parking lot.

Sandy watched them for a moment, then started laughing.

"Hey, you guys, put me down! How do you expect me to celebrate with you from up here?"

Matt Christopher®

Sports Bio Bookshelf

Muhammad Ali

Lance Armstrong

Kobe Bryant

Jennifer Capriati

Dale Earnhardt, Sr.

Jeff Gordon

Ken Griffey Jr.

Mia Hamm

Tony Hawk

Ichiro

Derek Jeter

Randy Johnson

Michael Jordan

Mario Lemieux

Mark McGwire

Yao Ming

Shaquille O'Neal

Jackie Robinson

Alex Rodriguez

Babe Ruth

Curt Schilling

Sammy Sosa

Venus and Serena
Williams

Tiger Woods

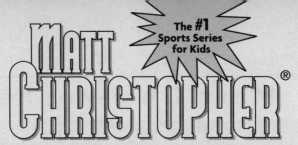

The #1 Sports Series for Kids

MATT CHRISTOPHER®

Read them all!

*Previously published as Crackerjack Halfback

All available in paperback from Little, Brown and Company

**Previously published as Pressure Play